READING CHAMPION

Stuck in the Mud

by Damian Harvey and Denis Cristo

Farmer Brown came out
of her house.

The rain had stopped
and the sun had come out.
"Look at all this mud,"
she said.

Farmer Brown

went to see Goat.

"Come on, Goat,"
said Farmer Brown.
But Goat did not get up.

"Oh, no!" said Farmer Brown.

"Goat is stuck in the mud."

Along came Old Tom.

"Can you help?"

said Farmer Brown.

He pushed and pushed.
But Goat was stuck
in the mud.

"Oh, no!" said Farmer Brown.

"Goat is stuck in the mud

and Old Tom is stuck in the mud."

Farmer Brown got the tractor.

"Oh, no!" she said.

"The tractor is stuck in the mud."

Along came Polly.

"Can you help?

said Farmer Brown.

"Goat is stuck in the mud.

Old Tom is stuck, too!"

Polly had a big apple.

"Come on, Goat," she said.

Goat got up.

"Goat was not stuck in the mud,"

said Polly.

"Oh, no!" said Farmer Brown
and Old Tom.
"We are stuck in the mud!"

Story trail

Start

Start at the beginning of the story trail. Ask your child to retell the story in their own words, pointing to each picture in turn to recall the sequence of events.

Independent Reading

This series is designed to provide an opportunity for your child to read on their own. These notes are written for you to help your child choose a book and to read it independently.

In school, your child's teacher will often be using reading books which have been banded to support the process of learning to read. Use the book band colour your child is reading in school to help you make a good choice. *Stuck in the Mud* is a good choice for children reading at Blue Band in their classroom to read independently.

The aim of independent reading is to read this book with ease, so that your child enjoys the story and relates it to their own experiences.

About the book
Farmer Brown discovers Goat is stuck in the mud. She tries to get Goat free but soon gets stuck herself!

Before reading
Help your child to learn how to make good choices by asking: "Why did you choose this book? Why do you think you will enjoy it?" Look at the cover together and ask: "What do you think the story will be about?" Support your child to think of what they already know about the story context. Read the title aloud and ask: "Where is the story set? What might get stuck in the mud?" Remind your child that they can try to sound out the letters to make a word if they get stuck. Decide together whether your child will read the story independently or read it aloud to you. When books are short, as at Blue Band, your child may wish to do both!

During reading

If reading aloud, support your child if they hesitate or ask for help by telling the word. Remind your child of what they know and what they can do independently.

If reading to themselves, remind your child that they can come and ask for your help if stuck.

After reading

Use the story trail to encourage your child to retell the story in the right sequence, in their own words.

Support comprehension by asking your child to tell you about the story. Help your child think about the messages in the book that go beyond the story and ask: "How would you help Farmer Brown? Why do you think the goat moved so easily at the end of the story?" Give your child a chance to respond to the story: "Did you have a favourite part? What words best describe the goat?

Extending learning

Help your child understand the story structure by using the same sentence patterns and adding different elements. For example, Dog is stuck in a hole. "Oh no!" said Milly, "Dog is stuck in a hole." Along came Joe. "Can you help?". Ask your child to describe what could happen next?

In the classroom, your child's teacher may be reinforcing punctuation and how it informs the way we group words in sentences. On a few of the pages, ask your child to find the speech marks that show us where someone is talking and then read it aloud, making it sound like talking. Find the question marks and exclamation marks and ask your child to practise the expression they used for questions and exclamations.

Franklin Watts
First published in Great Britain in 2017
by The Watts Publishing Group

Series Editors: Jackie Hamley and Melanie Palmer
Series Advisors: Dr Sue Bodman and Glen Franklin
Series Designer: Peter Scoulding

A CIP catalogue record for this book is
available from the British Library.

ISBN 978 1 4451 5483 1(hbk)
ISBN 978 1 4451 5484 8 (pbk)
ISBN 978 1 4451 6094 8 (library ebook)

Printed in China

Franklin Watts
An imprint of
Hachette Children's Group
Part of The Watts Publishing Group
Carmelite House
50 Victoria Embankment
London EC4Y 0DZ

An Hachette UK Company
www.hachette.co.uk

www.franklinwatts.co.uk

FSC
www.fsc.org
MIX
Paper from
responsible sources
FSC® C104740